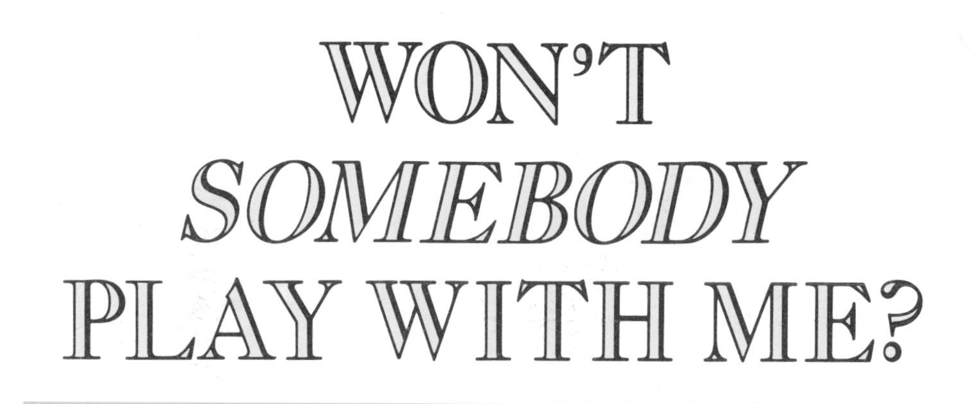

STORY AND PICTURES BY

STEVEN KELLOGG

A PUFFIN PIED PIPER

 Library of Congress Catalog Card Number: 72-708
First Pied Piper Printing 1976
Printed in the USA.

10 9 8 7 6 5 4 3 2 1

WON'T *SOMEBODY* PLAY WITH ME? is published in a hardcover edition by
Dial Books for Young Readers, 375 Hudson Street, New York, New York 10014
ISBN 0-14-054729-0
Reprinted by arrangement with Dial Books For Young
Readers, a division of Penguin Books USA Inc.

OUT TO LUNCH
PRIVATE
KEEP
OUT
FOR
KIM

“Happy birthday, Kim!”
“When do we open the presents?”
“At five thirty when your daddy comes home from work.”

"While I'm waiting for five thirty,
I think I'll go down the hall to Timmy's apartment."

We can play witch and giant or famous generals or maybe we

can pretend that we have an orphanage for lost baby animals.

"Hello, Mrs. Lewis. Can Timmy come out?"

"I'm sorry, Kim, but Timmy has things to do inside for a while. He'll telephone you later when he's finished."

I have to have somebody to play with.
I'll go see if my friend Annie is home.

We can play superwomen or doctors or maybe we can run a famous

restaurant and serve pineapple pancakes with bubblegum sauce.

"Hello, Mrs. Schwartz. Can Annie come out?"

"I'm sorry, Kim, but Annie isn't here right now.
She's gone to Timmy's house for the day."

Timmy and Annie! They're probably over there playing witch and giant together!

I'll go to Philip's house.

We can play ape family or spies or maybe we can pretend

that we're fierce, fat dinosaurs munching on bones.

"Hello, Mrs. Orfiello. Can Philip come out?"

"I'm sorry, Kim, but Philip isn't here.
He went over to Timmy's house for the day."

Timmy and Annie and Philip! They're over there together!
I bet they're playing ape family. And there's no one to play with me.

Well, if I were a queen
sitting at a huge table
piled with desserts
and Timmy and Annie
and Philip knocked
on the door, I wouldn't
let them in! I'd just
sit there and stuff
myself!

A CHOCOLATE SUNDAE
KIM
QUEEN KIM Loves QUEEN KIM
HAPPY DAY TO DEAR ME
TONIGHT
QUEEN KIM
WILL GIVE
A
GRAND
PARTY
no one
is invited
except
The QUEEN And her
Teddy
Give me your lives
Please can't we play?

If I owned a toy store
filled with the best
toys in the world
and Timmy and Annie
and Philip knocked
on the door, I wouldn't
let them in. I'd just
play and play and play
by MYSELF!

LARGER PLAYHOUSES MAY BE ORDERED
CASTLES
CATHEDRALS AND AMPHITHEATERS
MANSIONS et CHATEAUX
PLAYHOUSES
BICYCLES
GOOD BOOKS
Games
BEACH TOYS
NO
CUCKOO HOUSE
TOUR THE SHOP ON OUR MAGIC ROLLER COASTER THEN: ORDER ONE FOR YOUR ROOM
YIPPEE! its on SALE
A GENUINE COVERED WAGON Buy now and a friendly team of oxen is included at the Bargain Price

If I had a rocket
and Timmy and Annie
and Philip called on
a walkie-talkie and said,
Can we come too?
I'd yell:
BLAST OFF!

And there I'd be...

all by myself…

alone.

But, boy, am I mad at Timmy!

And I'm really

mad at Annie!

That stupid Philip!

I might as well go home.

"Hello, Kim! How are you?"
"MAD!"
"Would you borrow a cup of sugar for me from Mrs. Lewis?"
"Do I have to?"

"Well, it's for your birthday cake."
"Okay."
21a

"Hello, Kim. We were just about to call you."

SURPRISE!
HAPPY BIRTHDAY
KIM the GREAT
HAPPY BIRTHDAY
To ANNIE'S PAL
KIM
LOVE FROM YOUR FRIEN
ANNI

About the Author-Artist

Steven Kellogg is well known for his books for young children. His *Can I Keep Him?* was selected as one of the Best Books of the Year 1971 by *School Library Journal*, and his interpretation of Hilaire Belloc's *Matilda Who Told Lies and Was Burned To Death* was chosen by *The New York Times* as one of the Best Illustrated Books of 1970. Among his other books are *The Mystery Beast of Ostergeest*, *The Orchard Cat*, *Won't* Somebody *Play With Me?*, *The Island of the Skog*, *The Mystery of the Missing Red Mitten*, and most recently, *Much Bigger Than Martin*. Mr. Kellogg lives in Sandy Hook, Connecticut.